Bear's Spooky Book of Hidden Things

GERGELY DUDÁS

HARPER

An Imprint of HarperCollins*Publishers*

To my little sister, Orsi

Bear's Spooky Book of Hidden Things
Copyright © 2018 by Gergely Dudás
All rights reserved. Manufactured in China.
No part of this book may be used or reproduced in any manner whatsoever without written
permission except in the case of brief quotations embodied in critical articles and reviews.
For information address HarperCollins Children's Books,
a division of HarperCollins Publishers, 195 Broadway, New York, NY 10007.
www.harpercollinschildrens.com

ISBN 978-0-06-257079-6

Typography by Alison Klapthor
18 19 20 21 22 SCP 10 9 8 7 6 5 4 3 2 1
❖
First Edition

Tonight is Halloween, and it's time to trick-or-treat with Bear
and have some spooky fun!
Bear loves all kinds of treats, but his favorite is honeycomb—
he hopes he gets lots of it.

Can YOU help Bear find this special treat at each of his Halloween parties?

To start, Bear's stopping by a party at the corn maze.

He's going to need a wagon to carry all his treats in!

CORN MAZE

Do YOU see a **red wagon** here?

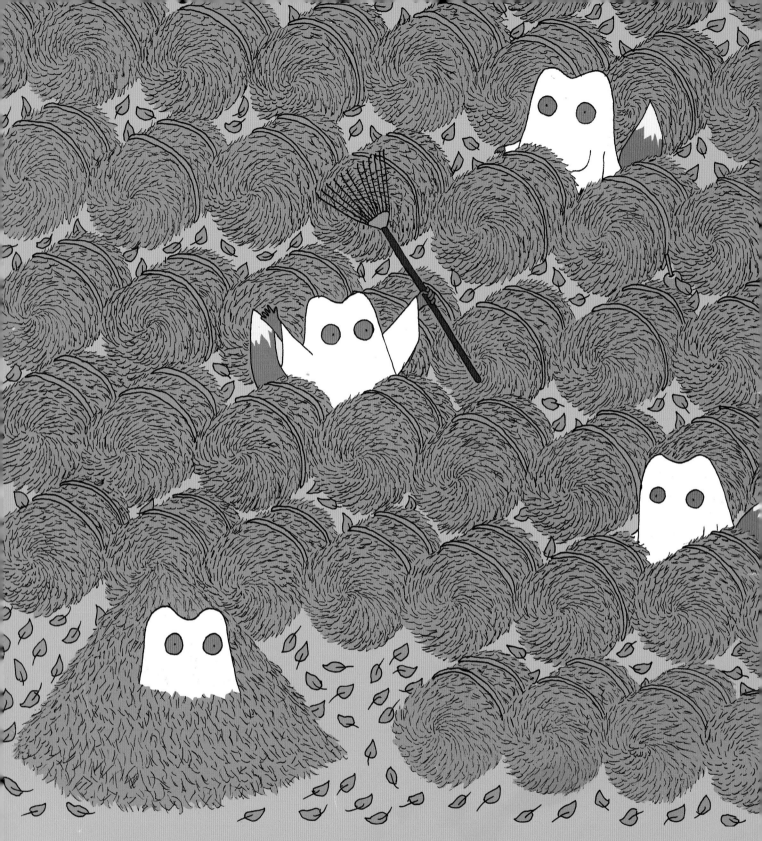

Bear's fox friends like caramel apples better than honeycomb.
Too bad for Bear!
Can YOU find a **caramel apple**?

Candy corn isn't quite as tasty as honeycomb—but Bear still likes it.

It's hard to tell the **candy corn** from the real corn!

Can YOU figure it out?

This party is getting spooky!
Bear is up to his eyeballs in—*ew!*—eyeballs.
Luckily, he heard the Frankenstein bunnies have a
delicious **lollipop** for him here. . . .

Bear's friends have lost their **witch's toad**.

And they even dressed up as toads to match!

Do YOU spy their little green pet?

Uh-oh, Bear is lost in the corn maze.

Luckily, there are plenty of signs! And one of them has letters

written in delicious **gummy worms**. But which one?

The moles think it wouldn't be Halloween without a **jack-o'-lantern**—and Bear agrees. Can YOU spot one?

The corn maze was a lot of fun. But no honeycomb!
Now Bear's off to trick-or-treat at the haunted house,

where they have some scary party favors: **spider rings**!
Can YOU see the one hidden here?

Every good haunted house has a haunted library.
And this haunted library has a **bottle of witch's brew** hidden on the shelves
Find it, quick—this place gives Bear the shivers!

Bear's raccoon friends dressed up as mad scientists.
There's no honeycomb in their lab, but
there *is* a mysterious **pocket watch**. Can YOU uncover it?

Spooky skeletons give Bear the willies.
Especially the **toy skull** in this pile of toy bones.
Yikes!

Halloween is all about costumes!

These goblin bunnies are looking for a **masquerade mask**
to add to their ensembles.

There's one here somewhere . . . but where?

By now, Bear has lots of treats . . . and yet still no honeycomb.
Maybe he'll get some at the pumpkin patch!

While Bear is looking for honeycomb, can YOU spot a **gourd**?

Everyone has their own favorite Halloween sweet, and the beaver family loves **donuts**. All these cobwebs make it hard to find one! Can YOU do it?

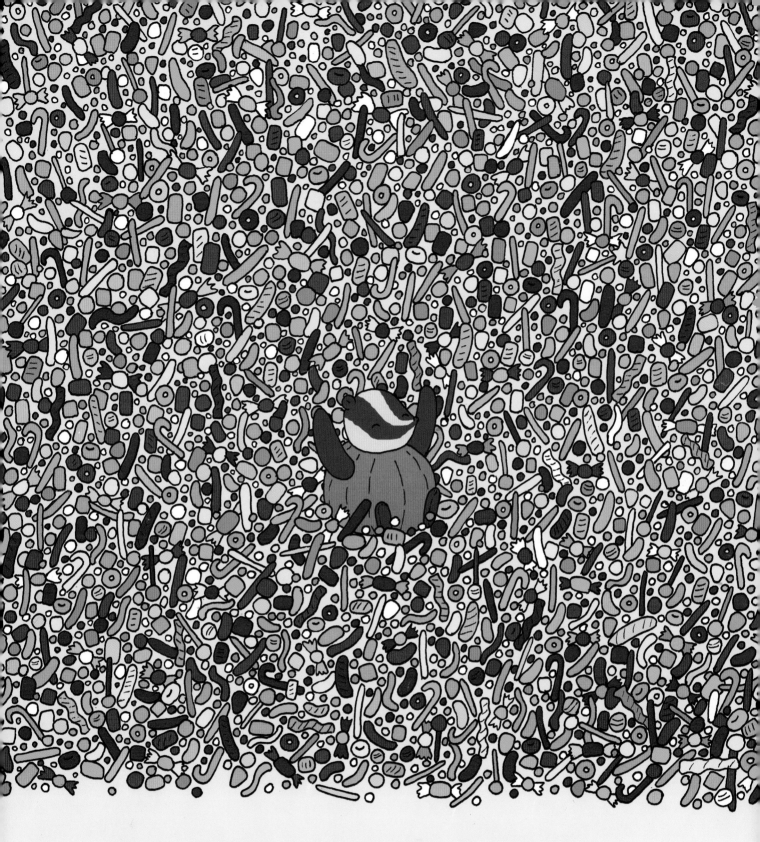

Bear's skunk friends have all kinds of candy for Bear.

But YOU need to look for a special **magic wand**!

Bear likes these colorful Halloween buckets,
and his groundhog friends tucked a pair of
wax lips among them. What a fun prize!

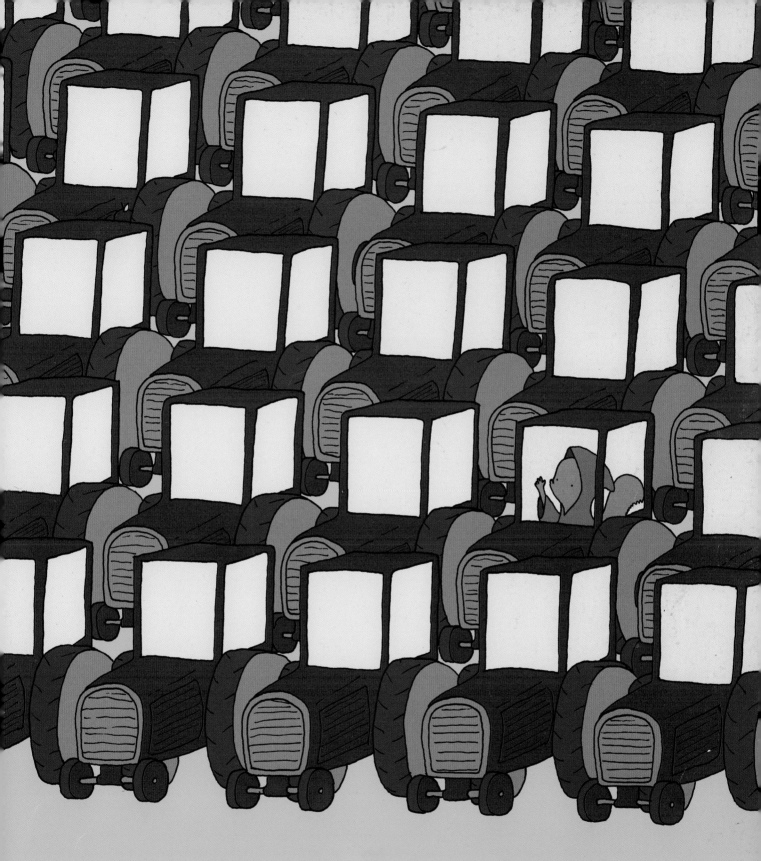

A pumpkin patch needs plenty of tractors, but this is getting ridiculous! How are you supposed to find a **red apple** here?

Bear's ready for his next party!

Will THIS one have honeycomb?

But first: Where's the **bag of candy** hidden in this forest?

Watch out, this old cemetery is full of witches!
Can YOU spot the extra **witch hat** for Bear to try on?

Bear's chipmunk friends are so excited about their bat costumes, none of them have noticed the **broomstick** among the tree branches. Have YOU?

The mice have crashed a kitten party!

Or maybe it's the other way around. . . .

Either way, can you spot the one **all-black cat**?

Are you ready to make the biggest find of Halloween night?

It's the **moon**!

(Although it's a little hard to see it with

all these crystal balls in the way. . . .)

Bear had fun at all the parties, even though he never found any honeycomb.

But wait! It looks like his friends found some for him!

And they're here for one last Halloween party . . . at Bear's house!

Happy Halloween, Bear!